William Cullen Bryant, Stephen Van C. White

Selections From the Portfolio of S. V. White

William Cullen Bryant, Stephen Van C. White

Selections From the Portfolio of S. V. White

ISBN/EAN: 9783337343637

Printed in Europe, USA, Canada, Australia, Japan

Cover: Foto ©Andreas Hilbeck / pixelio.de

More available books at **www.hansebooks.com**

THIS LITTLE VOLUME IS PUBLISHED

AND

AFFECTIONATELY DEDICATED

TO THE AUTHOR

BY

HIS DAUGHTER.

PHRENOCOSM.

READ AT THE ANNIVERSARY OF THE GNOTHAUTII, KNOX COLLEGE, JUNE 21, 1854.

WITHIN a dell where sparkling in the sun,
From clear sweet fountains, flashing waters run,
Whose purling dimples seemed by Nereids formed,
Whose flowery banks the Nereids' selves adorned ;
Where sighing soft the genii of the breeze
Breathed their sweet cadence thro' the leafy trees ;
Upon whose boughs in rich enamelled hue,
Hung the fair fruits which gods delight to view ;
Where through the rustling boughs the wand'ring eye
Meets here and there the vaulted azure sky,
Mid fleecy clouds where grouped in grandeur wild,
Shape upon shape the fairy forms were piled ;
There, where the spirits of the earth and sky
Seem in the rich embroidery to vie,

PHRENOCOSM.

There strayed a youth, whose thoughtful beaming face
Bespoke a soul which Genius deigned to grace,
Whose mind from nature as a book could learn,
The thought-forms, which shaped nature to discern.
And, as he gazed upon this fairy sight,
His senses wrapped in pure and calm delight,
Chained by a spell like wizard charm of yore,
His tranquil musings thus in numbers pour:
The world without us, all its forms how fair,
God's beauties blushing through the earth and air,
The diamond glittering in its pearly bed,
The gentle flowret lifting up its head,
The strong, resistless, ever heaving tide,
The storm-charged clouds that on the whirlwinds ride,
The planets wheeling through the rounds of space,
And myriad systems balanced each in place:
Or great, or small, alike their beauties show,
Dew-drops like suns in mimic splendor glow.
    But could some power propitious teach the art
To pour our eyesight on the mind or heart,
To paint our thoughts, or give emotions hue,
Till thoughts and passions stand revealed to view,

PHRENOCOSM.

Clad in a lustre that might praise command
Even from bright seraphs of the spirit land,
Compared, the world tho' fair in every form,
Would fade like starlight into coming morn.
When at Jehovah's voice the astonished earth
From out the dark abyss stood trembling forth,
When chaos from the scene abashed withdrew,
And over nothing her thick mantle threw,
When back the waters by the land were driven,
And myriad stars lit up the vault of heaven,
When from the dust a living form arose,
Omnipotence did but his power disclose,
Which into being spoke material forms,
And formed from naught whate'er our senses charms.
Not so was formed the ever living soul ;
Creation lost the act that crowned the whole.
Jehovah then from highest heaven descends
And o'er that lifeless form majestic bends ;
Breathed in his nostrils then the living flame ;
Touched with Promethean fire his lifeless frame.
Creation from the *hand* of God was given ;
The mind is an *afflatus* breathed from heaven.

PHRENOCOSM.

The mind whose subtle forms eye cannot see,
Simple amid its vast complexity,
'Tis as a harp of thousand hidden strings,
Unknown, save by the melody it brings;
A mechanism perfect in each part,
Which into motion e'en a breath can start;
Bound to material forms, its dwelling place,
By hidden links not e'en itself can trace.
Whence comes this subtle ever-living part,
Which moves in motion, pulsates in the heart?
Whence springs this quickening and immortal flame
Transfused throughout our dull decaying frame?
Eternal mystery its source enshrouds,
Like that of Egypt's river, wrapped in clouds.

How strange the union, strange the ties which bind
Essence and body, dust and living mind.
Go look upon the bent and trembling form
Bowed by the blasts of four-score Winters' storm,
Of one, who, like the giant of the wood,
Leafless and branchless, many a day hath stood;
Whose faltering footsteps totter o'er the grave
From which all human power not long can save;

PHRENOCOSM.

Whose eye o'er-worn, with life's protracted gaze
Can scarce distinguish e'en the sun's bright rays ;
Whose palsied hand nor deafened ear scarce brings
Or shape or sound from out material things ;
Dimmed every sense, yet still undimmed his mind,
His sight still clear, although his eye is blind ;
Though dark without, yet all ideal things
Flit shadowy by on visionary wings.
     The mind is as some castle, dim and vast,
Whose chambers are through countless portals passed ;
Where, lodged within each, in its proper cell,
The subtle parts of this vast system dwell.
Could we but enter where the memory stands
And guards the thought-forms treasured by his hands,
Could see the thousand hidden links that bind
Associations thousand cords could find—
The Sibyl's cave, in all its wonders dressed,
No such mysterious beauty e'er possessed.
Yon aged sire that marks his children's sport,
How yields his sad mood to each gay retort !
Waked by the merry shout, his boyhood stands
Crowned with a thousand joys at memory's hands ;

PHRENOCOSM.

Now glows his face flushed with the sudden joy ;
Once more he sports, once more himself a boy.
    The exile wanders o'er Siberia's snows,
Across the barren heath alone he goes,
The bleak winds whistle o'er that dreary waste,
And drifting snow-wreaths circle his cold face,
And save the snow-pile and the stunted fern
No object can his failing eye discern.
No object? Yes! There is! It must be so.
A rude built hut half buried 'neath the snow.
The exile nears it, and with heartfelt praise
To heaven, he seeks his earnest thanks to raise.
He goes within—that rude hut boasts no lock ;
No shutter bids the weary exile knock ;
But each rude gust that o'er the mountain blows,
Deposits there its freight of drifting snows.
A few burnt brands, whose fires are long since dead ;
A pile of turf that forms a scanty bed ;
The rude built walls and snow-bedrifted sides,
Are all the comforts which that hut provides.
Hope nerves the wandering exile's sinking frame ;
He seeks to kindle there the genial flame,

And while each nook for fuel now he tries,
A worn and tattered volume meets his eyes.
He takes it up, as from its page he reads,
Nor toil, nor cold, nor hunger now he heeds ;
Forgotten now the bitter biting cold ;
Remembered naught save that his chill hands hold.
"Oh, Poland ! 'Tis thy name, my native land !
Thy bleeding streams and battered walls here stand.
Oh hallowed volume ! Ceaseless be the fame
That bears the glorious Kosciusko's name."
How calm the exile now ; his mind, still free,
Visits his home in pleasing reverie.
No longer now an exile doomed to roam ;
Those rude built walls seem like his childhood's home;
Those wintry blasts that howl around his head
Are but the mountain winds that round him played
On Poland's rough and earthquake-riven face,
By memory clad in borrowed loveliness ;
A halo such as erst in childhood graced
The faded beauty of a mother's face.
Association thrills her hidden strings,
And fancy o'er the scene her magic flings.

Memory unlocks her storied treasures now ;
Pleasure once more lights up the exile's brow,
He sees again his father's manly form,
Whose strength has braved full many a winter's storm;
He hears again the song his mother sung
When first on his young ear those accents rung.
And still more near he dandles on his knee,
Heaven's surest pledge of earth's felicity ;
Presses the form close to his beating heart,
While from his lids the tears unbidden start,
Of her to whom his youthful love was given
Who bore the exile's fervent love to heaven.
Where lurked upon that leaf the secret power
That thrilled the exile in that dreary hour ?
And where the Lethean spell that thus should hide
Self and the pressing ills that self betide ?
Ah, look within and there the enchanter find,
See the magician in the exile's mind.

    See yonder where the rapturous speaker stands,
While the dense crowd his every look attends ;
A thousand ears catch the yet nascent word ;
A thousand hearts re-echo it when heard.

PHRENOCOSM.

He speaks of *home*—a thousand fancies start,
And scenes far distant press each labored heart
As bursts the lightning on the eye of night,
Quick as the meteor flashes on the sight,
A thousand cottages by magic rise ;
A thousand homes delight the listeners' eyes.
Where rise the bleak New England's rugged hills ;
Where low her vales, or gush her mountain rills ;
Where surge the billows and the hoarse winds roar ;
Where war the wild waves with the rock-girt shore ;
Or on the prairies, 'neath the setting sun,
Young nature's play-ground where she sportive run ;
Or 'neath the sunny sky of tropic clime ;
Or where Arcturus decks his fields with rime ;
There speed the thoughts on space-neglecting wings ;
There fancy hies and untold pleasure brings.
    The mind—who shall its limits dare define ?
Who fix its bounds, and who its cast design ?
While Newton slumbered on his mother's breast,
Without a thought, in semi-lifeless rest,
What wizard deep within that infant mind,
Germ of Principia's mighty truths could find ?

PHRENOCOSM.

Who could discern the power that e'en should draw
From nature's self her hidden wondrous law,
Which from the distant, wheeling orbs should find
The laws which all in one vast system bind?
 On Corsica, unknown a league around,
Unconscious lay the hero world-renowned;
Sleep, and the mother's milk his sole desire;
Unthinking then where lurked the secret fire.
Those secret passions which like storms should break,
Empires and kingdoms to their centres shake;
Europa's monarchs felt no secret fears;
No genii whispered warnings in their ears.
Why do they now as suppliants entreat
And prostrate bend before his haughty feet?
And why do thousands guard Helena's shore,
When Corsica knew not his natal hour?
The latent spark has kindled to a blaze—
The germ has burst, its heaven-high boughs to raise.
The infant oak lies prisoned in its cell
A mighty tree encrusted by a shell.
It bursts those walls, and upward seeks the sky;
Spreads wide its arms, whose strength the storms defy.

But while it seeks its heavenward boughs to throw,
The slow decay brings e'en its green head low ;
Now crumbling falls the monarch of the wood ;
Time lays that low which tempests long withstood.
Not so the soul—though grown to towering height,
Though knowledge sheds around a halo bright,
Though science has her storied treasures given,
That soul transplanted to the fields of heaven
Borne still aloft by heaven's celestial fire,
Its towering wing shall mount forever higher
Reflect the beauties of its bright abode,
And claim its kindred with its maker—God.

THE PLANTING OF THE APPLE-TREE.

WM. CULLEN BRYANT.

[When this poem first appeared in the *Atlantic Monthly*, the stanza in italics was written in honor of an unsung virtue of the apple-tree.]

COME, let us plant the apple-tree.
Cleave the tough greensward with the spade;
Wide let its hollow bed be made;
There gently lay the roots, and there
Sift the dark mould with kindly care,
 And press it o'er them tenderly,
As, round the sleeping infant's feet
We softly fold the cradle-sheet;
 So plant we the apple-tree.

PLANTING OF THE APPLE-TREE.

What plant we in this apple-tree?
Buds, which the breath of summer days
Shall lengthen into leafy sprays;
Boughs where the thrush, with crimson breast,
Shall haunt and sing and hide her nest;
  We plant, upon the sunny lea,
A shadow for the noontide hour,
A shelter from the summer shower,
  When we plant the apple-tree.

What plant we in this apple-tree?
Sweets for a hundred flowery springs
To load the May-wind's restless wings,
When, from the orchard row, he pours
Its fragrance through our open doors;
  A world of blossoms for the bee,
Flowers for the sick girl's silent room,
For the glad infant sprigs of bloom,
  We plant with the apple-tree.

PLANTING OF THE APPLE-TREE.

What plant we in this apple-tree?
Fruits that shall swell in sunny June,
And redden in the August noon,
And drop, when gentle airs come by,
That fan the blue September sky,
   While children come, with cries of glee,
And seek them where the fragrant grass
Betrays their bed to those who pass,
   At the foot of the apple-tree.

What plant we in the apple-tree?
Wine, which its hidden veins shall fill,
In golden crucibles distill,
And blushing from the gen'rous press,
Like maid at lover's fond caress,
   Shall flash to Heaven responsively
Gleams that were stolen from the sky,
When Jove prepared for feasts on high
   The nectar of the apple-tree.

PLANTING OF THE APPLE-TREE.

And when, above this apple-tree,
The winter stars are quivering bright,
And winds go howling through the night,
Girls, whose young eyes o'erflow with mirth,
Shall peel its fruit by cottage hearth,
   And guests in prouder homes shall see,
Heaped with the grape of Cintra's vine
And golden orange of the line,
   The fruit of the apple-tree.

The fruitage of this apple-tree
Winds, and our flag of stripe and star,
Shall bear to coasts that lie afar,
Where men shall wonder at the view
And ask in what fair groves they grew :
   And sojourners beyond the sea
Shall think of childhood's careless day
And long, long hours of summer play,
   In the shade of the apple-tree.

PLANTING OF THE APPLE-TREE.

Each year shall give this apple-tree
A broader flush of roseate bloom,
A deeper maze of verdurous gloom,
And loosen, when the frost-clouds lower,
The crisp brown leaves in thicker shower.
   The years shall come and pass, but we
Shall hear no longer, where we lie,
The summer's songs, the autumn's sigh,
   In the boughs of the apple-tree.

And time shall waste this apple-tree.
Oh, when its aged branches throw
Thin shadows on the ground below,
Shall fraud and force and iron will
Oppress the weak and helpless still?
   What shall the tasks of mercy be,
Amid the toils, the strifes, the tears
Of those who live when length of years
   Is wasting this apple-tree?

PLANTING OF THE APPLE-TREE.

"Who planted this old apple-tree?"
The children of that distant day
Thus to some aged man shall say;
And, gazing on its mossy stem,
The gray-haired man shall answer them:

"A poet of the land was he,
Born in the rude but good old times;
'Tis said he made some quaint old rhymes
On planting the apple-tree."

THE CURRICULUM OF LIFE!

[At a Summer Resort, it chanced that on August 1st, 1881, five birthdays of inmates of the house—aged respectively two, four, sixteen, fifty, and sixty-seven—were celebrated by a Dinner given by other guests.

The gentleman aged fifty, being called upon to respond on behalf of the AUGUST guests, after a few remarks, read the following lines, hurriedly composed by him for the occasion.]

I.

ROSY-FINGERED Aurora,—the old poets say,—
Erst opened, at dawning, the gates of the day,
And Phœbus led out, wild-champing to run,
The steeds that should draw forth the car of the Sun :
While the Hours, all attentive, in line took their place,
Obsequious, to mark every turn in the race.

II.

You all know the fable :—Now labor the steeds,
While the steeps of the East their swift running impedes.
Now open broad vistas, entrancing to view,
While Phœbus guides safe thro' the deep vault of blue ;
Lo! rivers, and mountains, and oceans unroll,
Euphrates a thread, and Olympus a mole.

III.

THE fleet-footed coursers sweep on, and full soon,
The chariot is poised on the crest of high noon ;
And far in the West, lies the home of the night,
Whose robes, like a pall, shall extinguish the light.
Apollo himself, strives in vain to delay,
The chariot's descent, to the death of the day !

IV.

How the dream of the Poet foreshadows our life !
The morning how arduous ! how earnest the strife !
How the wheels are weighed down in their courses, before
The baby of TWO, is the prattler of FOUR !
While the vista that opens to eyes of SIXTEEN,
Gives the mountain its blue, the river its sheen.

THE CURRICULUM OF LIFE.

V.

As I stand at the nooning of manhood to-day,
Looking forward and backward, o'er life's rugged way,
Recalling the past, with its visions of Love,
And piercing the future, with Hope from above ;
Let furrows of care from this brow flee away,
Silver hairs turn to golden, this FIFTIETH day !

VI.

LIKE the sun when majestic, he sinks to his rest,
And gilds with his rays every cloud in the West,
May Faith, as a gleam from the portals of Heaven,
Make radiant the face of THREE-SCORE-AND-SEVEN.
May Youth, Age, and Manhood, alike come to rest
In the morning that dawns, in the realm of the blest.

DIES IRÆ.

Dies Iræ, dies illa,
Solvet sæclum in favillâ,
Teste David cum Sibyllâ.

Day of wrath! O day appalling ;
Melts the earth, to ashes falling,
Prophet's words, and seer's recalling.

Quantus tremor est futurus,
Quando judex est venturus,
Cuncta stricte discussurus !

Oh ! what terror is impending,
See, the mighty Judge descending,
Laying bare each fault offending.

DIES IRÆ.

Tuba mirum spargens sonum
Per sepulchra regionum,
Coget omnes ante Thronum.

Trumpet wakes the slumb'ring legions
From the graves of all the regions,
At the Throne compels allegiance.

Mors stupebit, et Natura,
Cum resurget creatura,
Judicanti responsura.

Dazed is death, and trembles Nature,
When aghast—with pallid feature,—
Stands in judgment, every creature.

Liber scriptus proferetur,
In quo totum continetur.
Unde mundus judicetur.

Opened are the written pages
Which record the sins of ages.
Thence decreed are error's wages.

DIES IRÆ.

Judex ergo cum sedebit,
Quidquid latet apparebit ;
Nil inultum remanebit.

To that book the Judge appealing,
Every hidden thing revealing ;
Nothing arc we now concealing.

Quid sum, miser, tunc dicturus,
Quem patronum rogaturus,
Cum vix justus sit securus ?

What am I,—the wretched—saying ?
To what saint or angel praying,
When on just ones sins are weighing ?

Rex tremendæ majestatis,
Qui salvandos salvas gratis
Salva me, Fons pietatis.

King, majestic beyond measure,
Free to save of Thy good pleasure,
Give salvation as my treasure.

DIES IRÆ.

Recordare, Jesu pie,
Quod sum causa Tuæ viæ,
Ne me perdas illâ die.

Jesus, hear my supplication,
Since I caused Thine incarnation,
On that day, O grant salvation.

Quærens me, sedisti lassus,
Redemisti, crucem passus ;
Tantus labor non sit cassus.

Seeking me, Thou weary liest ;
To redeem me, lo! Thou diest ;
In thy labor fail not, Highest !

Juste Judex ultionis,
Donum fac remissionis,
Ante diem rationis.

Judge ! Thou just in retribution,
Make the gift of absolution
Ere the day of execution.

DIES IRÆ.

Ingemisco tanquam reus,
Culpâ rubet vultus meus,
Supplicanti parce, Deus.

Hear me groan, in anguish crushing,
Crimson faced from guilty blushing,
Spare me, all my terror hushing.

Qui Mariam absolvisti,
Et latronem exaudisti,
Mihi quoque spem dedisti.

Thou didst pardon Mary, needing;
Thou didst heed the robber's pleading,
And dost give me hope exceeding.

Preces meæ non sunt dignæ,
Sed tu bonus fac benigne,
Ne perenni cremer igne.

All unworthy is my praying,
Gracious One! Thy love displaying,
In endless fires forbid my staying.

DIES IRÆ.

Inter oves locum præsta,
Et ab hædis me sequestra.
Statuens in parte dextrâ.

Among the sheep, O Lord! instate me;
From the goats, O separate me;
With the blessed grant to rate me.

Confutatis maledictis,
Flammis acribus addictis,
Voca me cum benedictis.

When the damned from Thee are driven;
And to sharpest flames are given;
Call me to a home in Heaven.

Oro supplex et acclinis,
Cor contritum, quasi cinis;
Gere curam mei finis.

A suppliant, I kneel, imploring,
Crushed in heart, my grief outpouring,
Bear me to Thy throne, adoring.

DIES IRÆ.

Lacrymosa dies illa,
Quâ resurget ex favillâ
Judicandus homo reus.
Huic ergo parce, Deus.

Oh ! that dreadful day of weeping,
When man rising from his sleeping ;
For the Judgment must prepare him ;
Spare him, Lord, O kindly spare him.

Pie Jesu Domine,
Dona eis requiem sempiternam.

Jesus, Lord ! in love Supernal,
Give to him Thy rest eternal.